PONDLARKER

FRED GWYNNE

SIMON & SCHUSTER BOOKS FOR YOUNG READERS

New York • London • Toronto • Sydney • Tokyo • Singapore

SIMON & SCHUSTER BOOKS FOR YOUNG READERS
Simon & Schuster Building
Rockefeller Center
1230 Avenue of the Americas
New York, New York 10020

Manufactured in the United States of America

10   9   8   7   6   5   4   3   2

(pbk)   10   9   8   7   6   5   4   3   2   1

Library-of-Congress Cataloging-in-Publication Data
Gwynne, Fred.
Pondlarker / written and illustrated by Fred Gwynne.
p.   cm.
SUMMARY: Not satisfied being a frog. Pondlarker seeks
a princess' kiss to fulfill his princely ambitions.
[1. Fairy tales.   2. Frogs—Fiction.   3. Self-acceptance—
Fiction.]   I. Title.
PZ8.G98Po   1990
[E]—dc20   90-9524
                                     CIP
                                     AC

ISBN 0-671-70846-5   ISBN 0-671-77818-8 (pbk)

"No longer was he a frog, but a handsome
young prince with beautiful kind eyes."

Pondlarker's favorite story

Once upon a time, when there were more princes in the world than anything else...

...there was a family of frogs who lived in a pond.
A mother and father and all their children.

Every night, before the children went to sleep, their mother read them a story about a princess and a frog.

Maybe you know it.

It's the story of the princess who kisses a frog and turns him into a prince.

Well, as you can imagine, it was their favorite story of all.

And, for years, they believed it was true.

But, as time went by, and the young frogs grew older and went to work and got married and settled down and had families of their own, they soon forgot such childish things.

Except for one of them, that is. His name was Pondlarker.

Pondlarker never forgot the story, and was always on the lookout for a princess to kiss him.

He dressed like a prince. He walked like a prince. He even thought he was one at times.

It got to be laughable.

Finally one day his mother and father sat Pondlarker down and had a heart-to-heart talk with him.

"There's nothing wrong with being a frog," advised his mother. "In fact there is everything right with being a frog."

Then Pondlarker's father sang him a song.

"Frogs long jump and dive
  Like no prince alive.
  We sing and we croak
  And swim every stroke
  From no stroke at all,
  To Australian crawl.
  We've got bigger lungs,
  Catch flies on our tongues,
  And do many things
  Much better than kings!"

But Pondlarker's mind was made up. And nothing was about to change it.

So one day when Pondlarker happened to see a sign that read, "PRINCESS 4 MILES," he up and left the pond behind him.

Pondlarker was little aware of the dangers that lurked ahead.

This way →

Now that way ←

He'd only walked a mile or two when a red-shouldered hawk swooped down at him from out of the sky.

With all the princely bearing at his command, Pondlarker quickly drew himself up, unsheathed his sword, and yelled "En garde!" Such gallant behavior from such a tiny individual so confused the hawk that he withdrew from battle and flew away.

A few miles further on it was a hungry mink that tried to do Pondlarker in.

Again Pondlarker bravely stood his ground, and calmly warned the mink that he, Pondlarker, would soon be a prince.

"And remember," he cautioned, "we princes wear *mink*-lined robes!"

The mink took the frog's warning to heart and quietly slunk away.

Sheathing his sword once more, Pondlarker continued to follow the signs that led to the princess.

Soon a castle appeared in the distance, and over the entrance was a sign that read "All Frogs Enter Here."

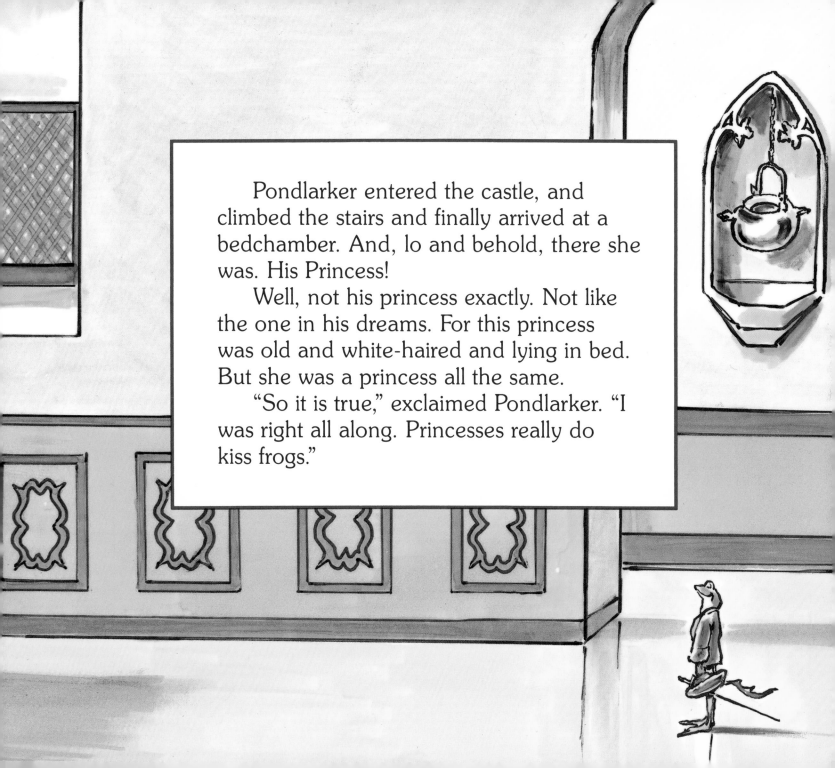

Pondlarker entered the castle, and climbed the stairs and finally arrived at a bedchamber. And, lo and behold, there she was. His Princess!

Well, not his princess exactly. Not like the one in his dreams. For this princess was old and white-haired and lying in bed. But she was a princess all the same.

"So it is true," exclaimed Pondlarker. "I was right all along. Princesses really do kiss frogs."

"Oh, my, yes," sighed the princess. "I've kissed millions of frogs. I've kissed bullfrogs, wood frogs, cricket frogs, carpenter frogs, white-lipped frogs, whistling frogs, gopher frogs, pig frogs, pickerel frogs, leopard frogs, sheep frogs, peepers...oh, dear me, so many kinds of frogs.

"Sad to say, though, I've never found a prince that was good enough for me! They either turned out to be too fat or too thin or too young or too old or too tall or too short or too boring...or too something.

"But enough talk," she said. "Come and let me kiss you. Maybe you'll turn out to be my Prince Charming."

And then, with a slight smile, she added, "Even if it turns out that you aren't my Prince Charming, at least there'll be one less slimy frog in the world. And that's a good thing, I'm sure you agree."

But Pondlarker wasn't so sure that he did agree. There was nothing wrong with being a frog. In fact, as his mother had said, "There is everything right with being a frog."

And, maybe, if you really want to think about it, there was a little bit of prince in Pondlarker already. Hadn't he defended himself against the hawk and outsmarted the mink as bravely as any prince? Not only that. Wasn't it also true that Pondlarker could do lots of things that princes couldn't? Like long jumping and croaking and catching flies on his tongue. All the things that his father had sung about.

Suddenly, before the princess could kiss him, Pondlarker shed his clothes and jumped out the window into the moat below. It was a three hundred and fifty foot dive that would have terrified any prince. But it didn't bother Pondlarker one bit. He hit the water happy as any frog who had just seen the light.

And all the way back to the pond he sang his father's song. The hills echoed with, "We've got bigger lungs, catch flies on our tongues, and do many things much better than kings!"

Pondlarker finally settled down in the pond, and did do many things much better than kings.

He raised a wonderful family of four hundred and sixty children and ninety-two grandchildren. He gave each and every last one of them the very same advice that his mother had once given him. And every night he sang them his father's song. Maybe you've heard some of Pondlarker's grandchildren sing the song to *their* grandchildren.

In any case, it's no wonder there are so many frogs in the world today.

And so few princes.